Tirocchi

PUFFIN BOOKS
Published by the Penguin Group
Penguin Putnam Books for Young Readers, 345 Hudson Street, New York, New York, 10014, U.S.A.
Penguin Books Ltd, 27 Wrights Lane, London W8 5TZ, England
Penguin Books Australia Ltd, Ringwood, Victoria, Australia
Penguin Books Canada Ltd, 10 Alcorn Avenue, Toronto, Ontario, Canada M4V 3B2
Penguin Books (N.Z.) Ltd, 182–190 Wairau Road, Auckland 10, New Zealand
Penguin Books Ltd, Registered Offices: Harmondsworth, Middlesex, England

First Published in the United States of America by Puffin Books,
a division of Penguin Putnam Books for Young Readers, 2001

3 5 7 9 10 8 6 4

Text copyright © Harriet Ziefert, 2001
Illustrations copyright © Renée Andriani, 2001
All rights reserved

Puffin Books ISBN 0–14–056820–4

Printed in Hong Kong

ON HALLOWEEN NIGHT

by **Harriet Ziefert**

pictures by **Renée Andriani**

PUFFIN BOOKS

This is Halloween night.

This is the cape that grandma brought
for Emily to wear on Halloween night.

This is the skirt that grandpa bought...
To go with the cape that grandma brought
for Emily to wear on Halloween night.

These are socks with stripes on the side...
To go with the skirt that grandpa bought...
To go with the cape that grandma brought
for Emily to wear on Halloween night.

This is a purse with the strings untied...
To go with the socks with stripes on the side...
To go with the skirt that grandpa bought...
To go with the cape that grandma brought
    for Emily to wear on Halloween night.

This is a hat with a big, black rim...
To go with the purse with the strings untied...
To go with the socks with stripes on the side...
To go with the skirt that grandpa bought...
To go with the cape that grandma brought
   for Emily to wear on Halloween night.

This is a snake that's long and slim...
To go with the hat with a big, black rim...
To go with the purse with the strings untied...
To go with the socks with stripes on the side...
To go with the skirt that grandpa bought...
To go with the cape that grandma brought
   for Emily to wear on Halloween night.

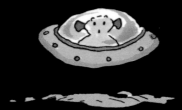

These are bracelets that rattle and clack...
To go with the snake that's long and slim...
To go with the hat with a big, black rim...
To go with the purse with the strings untied...

To go with the socks with stripes on the side...
To go with the skirt that grandpa bought...
To go with the cape that grandma brought
    for Emily to wear on Halloween night.

This is a necklace all twisty and black...
To go with the bracelets that rattle and clack...
To go with the snake that's long and slim...
To go with the hat with a big, black rim...
To go with the purse with the strings untied...

To go with the socks with stripes on the side...
To go with the skirt that grandpa bought...
To go with the cape that grandma brought
    for Emily to wear on Halloween night.

This is the costume that Emily wore
on Halloween night.

This is the bell that Emily rang...
This is the boy who answered the bell
that Emily rang on Halloween night.

This is the treat that came from the boy
who answered the bell that Emily rang
on Halloween night.

This is a happy Halloween night!

Harriet Ziefert is the author of many children's books, including *Halloween Parade*.

Renée Andriani is the illustrator of the Shawn and Keeper books.